Bhuwaneshwar

WOLVES
and
Other
Stories

TRANSLATED BY SAUDAMINI DEO

Seagull
BOOKS

LONDON NEW YORK CALCUTTA

Seagull Books, 2021

This compilation © Seagull Books, 2021

First published in English translation by Seagull Books, 2021

English translation and Introduction © Saudamini Deo, 2021

ISBN 978 0 8574 2 793 9

British Library Cataloguing-in-Publication Data
A catalogue record for this book is available from the British Library.

Typeset by Seagull Books, Calcutta, India
Printed and bound by WordsWorth India, New Delhi, India

Contents

TRANSLATOR'S INTRODUCTION

The Surrealists were known for their *Séance de rêve éveillé* or 'waking-dream sessions' where, influenced by the developing field of neuropsychology, they sought to unlock the terra incognita of the mind. In 1891, advertisements appeared in American newspapers of the magical talking-board game of Ouija, promising a link between 'the known and unknown, the material and immaterial.' It was perhaps with one of the early mass-produced planchette boards that my grandmother and her friends, and then later my mother and her friends, in the dimly lit rooms of Jodhpur, also attempted to contact the dead. Mediumship was popular too, where 'spirit mediums' use their bodies as the contact point between the living and the dead such that it is impossible to know where the medium begins and the spirit ends, where truth begins and performance ends. Translating Bhuwaneshwar is my *séance de rêve éveillé*. It is my contact with the dead genius of Hindi literature.

Bhuwaneshwar was born some time between 1910 and 1915 in Shahjahanpur, Uttar Pradesh. His mother died when he was about a year old; his father remarried a woman named Chameli Devi who apparently mistreated her stepson for the rest of his life.

Things got worse after a beloved uncle died from the plague. Growing up amid poverty and neglect, Bhuwaneshwar took to spending most of his time in his room, staring at the walls. A schoolteacher remembers him as a quiet boy, always writing or reading like a philosopher, never upto any mischief except for his secret cigarette habit. As he grew older, he acquired a reputation as something of a wit. Once when he paid a visit to Dr Dinesh Dwivedi, the physician's father said, 'Here, Dinesh, a patient has come.' 'I'm not a patient,' Bhuwaneshwar retorted, 'I'm a disease— I'm here to afflict.'

After school, Bhuwaneshwar never enrolled in college, and preferred to spend most of his teenage years visiting friends in other cities. Finally, in 1933, he was discovered by an unlikely mentor, Premchand, whose literary and social aesthetics could not have been more different than his protégé's, and yet it was he who published his stories in the eminent literary magazine *Hans*. A busy period of literary activity followed, with the publication of Bhuwaneshwar's first book, a collection of one-act plays (*Karwaan*) and the completion of a manuscript of English poems, *Words of Passage*. In 1936, at the inaugural speech of the Indian Progressive Writers' Association, Premchand declared Bhuwaneshwar to be the future of Hindi literature, if only he would temper his bitterness a little. Two years later, in 1938, Bhuwaneshwar wrote 'Wolves', one of his most important short stories.

For a writer who had expected to remain overlooked, his literary success may have proved too much to bear. It certainly proved too much for the literary community which—according to Rajkumar Sharma—seemed to embark on 'a cold war' against him. Suddenly, none of his writings were published any more. This hostility could partly be explained by the ingrained moral and social codes that Bhuwaneshwar and his works insisted on shattering. His writing questioned the very basis of society, insisting only on the primal truth. As Premchand wrote: 'Bhuwaneshwar has brought to light our secrets, our perversions with such brutality that one is scared to look at them.'

Completely dependent on the income from his writing, this literary hostility subjected him to another period of poverty and he took to spending his nights either at his friends's homes or on park benches or in vacant first-class train compartments. During 1941–42, the hostility subsided a little, enough for three of his short stories to be published, followed by the brilliant one-act play *Taambe Ka Keeda* ('The Copper Insect'). However, after a rejected marriage proposal and continuing financial problems, he slowly descended into alcoholism. This is when he began to live with his friend Suresh Awasthi and his brother, Girish, in Lukhnow. Suresh soon moved to Delhi but kept sending money home for his brother and Bhuwaneshwar. Then one evening, Girish began to scream and rushed out of the house. When he was found a few days later, he had to be taken to the Agra asylum where he spent the rest of his life.

Bhuwaneshwar had no choice, then, but to move out. And to go back to living at the railway station. His friends tried to help him, and brought him to Allahabad but an inability to assimilate into domestic environments doomed him to homelessness. It was in 1955 that a friend found him on the streets, clearly mentally unstable. When the friend tried to take him home, Bhuwaneshwar complained to the people around him that he was being harassed by a stranger. He spent his remaining days in Allahabad, and then, one day, went missing.

In October 1964, Laxmikant Verma wrote in the literary magazine *Ka-Kha-Ga*:

> Bhuwaneshwar is no more. It cannot be said with certainty whether he is dead or no more despite being alive. However, hundreds and thousands of inches of the blue electricity wires, which he used to wrap around his trousers in place of a belt and as laces on his shoes, are being sold even today in Allahabad. Ripped shirt, dirty and torn trousers, khaki almost greasy English tie, and on top of it all, in winter, a ripped Chesterfield coat and, in monsoon, a raincoat, a body turned dirty-dark due to not being bathed in years, remind us of that talent. Some people called him 'thief', some 'mad', some 'genius' and some even 'beggar', but in reality he possessed such a human personality that, after glimpsing the naked face of man, he himself broke, shattered.
>
> It is assumed that he died sometime in 1957. He was last spotted perhaps in Banaras, near the Dashashwamedh Ghat, ill and among the beggars.
>
> Bhuwaneshwar's story seems to have been much like the ones he loved to write; in its unfolding, it reminds us that life, no matter what, will evaporate into the nothingness of an untraceable dream. The wolves of our certain fate are approaching. The wolves will eat us, in the end.

The dark and dingy lanes kept filling with the monotonous, violent sound of the flaming wind against the tall damp buildings.

The fat, boorish doctor and the thin, sickly student Vilaas were silently walking hand-in-hand along the slippery verge. To avoid the mud, they were constantly hopping like frogs. Suddenly Vilaas' feet touched the slush and he screamed impatiently, 'Doctor, you are dead, absolutely dead, nothing more than that. Do you know you are dead? . . . I love you so much but what difference does that make? You are dead.'

'Okay, okay,' the doctor replied absently, supporting him with his arms.

'I'm being honest with you because I love you. Do you know how much I love you?'

'Yes, yes . . . of course I know . . .'

'This is hell, doctor, hell! A colony of the dead. This bustling city is a colony of the dead. Sometimes I think it is completely empty . . . this is not a city, this is a phantom. Doctor, is it possible that this cursed city is full of thousands of people who exist only to eat and drink and sleep? Darkness, muck, wind, rain. Look around, is there even a faint sign of life anywhere? No. Turn around and see. Will anyone believe that this is a city filled with people—alive, fully human, is this what is called humanity? . . . Why are they living? Why do mothers bear the pain of childbirth? . . . Imagine this colony disappeared, wiped off the face of the earth! Like a pile of cow dung washed away by the rain. It will make no difference to the world. No one will even know that a heap of cow dung is gone. And why should anyone know . . . a few clerks, shop-keepers, officers—every city has the same few clerks, shopkeepers, pimps, officers, exactly the same. Why are there so many duplicates when the original itself is despicable? Maybe the rain is falling exactly like this in many places, the wind is hissing exactly like this . . . doctor . . . doesn't even this make you despair? Not even this?'

'No-o. Why should I despair?' said the doctor, tired and out of breath from the 'labour' of supporting Vilaas.

'Hffff. Doesn't anything make you angry? It's because you're a corpse—you're dead.'

'I say this myself.'

'You only say it—you don't feel it. Do you feel that, despite being alive, you are slowly rotting, decaying like a corpse? *We are all decaying with little patience—little patience.* We should have gone to the cremation ground long ago.'

'Yes indeed, a very long time ago', the doctor replied even more absent-mindedly.

'I don't understand how you are alive—this is death, doctor death!'

'Death?'

Vilaas walked a few more steps, then jolted out of the doctor's hands and nearly fell. He recovered and leant against a damp wall in order to continue.

'I don't know—I don't know how anyone can live without having a *compelling contract* with life.'

'One cannot but one does anyway,' said the doctor, really bored now.

'We live? We are not living. We keep rotting like corpses. Our blood keeps turning into water through a cruel *conspiracy* and you call this life? You are polluting the environment. You call this life? Living things wither at your touch. You call this life, doctor?' Vilas carried on while trying to hold the doctor's hand with his characteristic irritability. 'Who can call this life? . . . Doctor, I don't have any money, not a cigarette . . . not even a book that I can sell, so I drink . . . and now? Doctor, don't I know that after this there is the endless apocalypse?'

'What is this nonsense!' the doctor both reprimanded and reassured him.

They both began to crawl through the dark again. The cold flames of wind whipped about abruptly. Over wet roofs and dark streets, clouds were climbing the sky like dust-cranes . . . higher . . . higher. Vilaas slipped in the mud over and over again. If the doctor hadn't caught him, he would have fallen at the turning. The doctor was really tired from supporting Vilaas' entire weight on his left arm—so tired that in a second everything started to seem unreal, dream-like. He realized that Vilaas' hand, which had been in his, was now raised rather high and he was almost being dragged behind him, but he was exhausted and that house had brought a strange ugliness to his mind. To ease his arm, he raised Vilaas' even higher, causing Vilaas to stumble and fall. 'Doctor,' it was as if the stumble had shaken his mind, 'Come, let's renounce the world, let's renounce it like the Buddha . . . hmph—come, let's sacrifice the world on the altar of a false god.' Vilaas was now slurring . . . 'but it's just that I love this world so! Doctor, you know how much I love you . . . but you are dead . . .'

Startled, the doctor replied, 'Shut up,' but then started sobbing . . . slowly . . . slowly . . . like a child.

Vilaas removed his hand from the doctor's, 'I love it! This world doesn't care for Vilaas, Vilaas has ruined his life, he plays no part in the commerce of the world. But Vilaas loves the innumerable proleta-proletariat of this world, because he has to live, he has to survive.' He held the doctor's hand again, who had unknowingly collided with him. He pressed the doctor's hand solemnly. Lowering his face to the doctor's, he murmured in a beguiling voice, 'Doctor, do you understand that we have to live? We must live, night's festivities are over, and we people are lying on the ground snuffed out like paper lamps. But you'll see, we people will flicker again, doctor, doctor!' The doctor was still sobbing, he was very weary. Vilaas, defeated, silently walked on. At a distance, a wave of dawn had scattered a shapeless cloud on a wet roof. In front, the red municipality lamp radiated smoke. Like an eye. A sticky, swollen eye in which the glare of light causes a bead of blood to appear. Vilaas screamed at the sight, 'Look, this is the light of the new world, that world for which we will live.' And he bowed to the light, folding one leg and two hands in the same way he had seen the sun worshippers do in his history books.

But the doctor was sobbing still, like a child, like a very weary child.

A GLIMPSE OF LIFE

Hair has turned grey. Two of my front teeth now useless. But no wrinkles on my body yet. Sixty-five years, six months, two days of my life have passed, today is the third day. My head aches slightly. When I was young, I had visited a palm-reader in Kashi. He said, 'You will live for sixty-five years, six months, three days.' According to his prediction, today is the last day of my life. I, too, believe that my life-force will flee my body today. Today I will be released from this magic-mansion. I have seen the world and seen it well. Till recently, I lived a comfortable life. I had a host of followers. I had contacts in high places. The whole city sang my praises; however, now my closest, most inseparable friends have dissolved like camphor into unknown air. My relatives—who used to visit me at least once a month—have refused to recognize me in these past years. If I run into them somewhere, they pass me by with lowered heads. Those who were my yes-men now run away from my very shadow. But I am still happy. I don't have material comforts but the heart is content. I don't get enough to eat, and yet I am happier than many affluent, prosperous people. The centre of my happiness is that goddess on whose left thigh I am resting my head. She has supported me through good times and bad; indeed, she is even more loving in this time of despair. She is my wife. I have been married for forty-five years. She has always made me happy, and I have also always tried to make her happy.

Today, as I am counting my last breaths, many scenes from the past pass before my eyes. Each event of my life is happening once again for the first time. I was the only son of my parents. I grew up rather spoilt. Father never raised his voice at me. I don't remember but Ma used to tell me that once she had slapped me. I cried for hours. When Father returned, he admonished Ma, and only then I stopped crying. After some time, I was sent away to study. I wasn't a bad student. I always stood first or second in class. There is one notable incident from that time. I had just entered adolescence. My heart was filled with joy, the whole world looked green. I grew close to a young girl. I loved her a lot. She loved me a lot as well. My emotions were pure. I didn't love in order to possess—but I did love her. She was my age. Highly intelligent. Perhaps it was her intelligence that attracted me. She wasn't really pretty. I have still not been able to forget her. I don't know if she is alive or dead. It's my deepest desire that she be happy. Slowly, our closeness was deepening into love. I had now gained the power of thought. I used to think that we would be very happy if we got married. I cannot forget that one particular day. Each detail from that time is clear before my eyes. We were alone. I was standing, and she was standing in front of me. We were arm wrestling with both arms. We used to play together regularly, but that day I felt a strange tingling all over my body when I placed my hands in hers. Like electricity coursing through my veins. I removed my hands from her hands. When I looked at her, I noticed her cheeks had turned a faint pink I couldn't understand this sudden transformation. She had just set foot in adolescence. There was talk of arranging her marriage. I wanted her to be married to me. Maybe she also wanted to marry me but neither of us said anything to each other. Love was never expressed. This was a silent love. She got married. Not to me—to another. I was poor. Her parents probably never even considered me as a groom—but no one apart from us knew how deeply happy she would have been with me. Her husband was good looking. I used to think she was happy. I contented myself with thoughts of her happiness. But I was under an illusion, she was not happy—her days were being spent in anguish. Her suffering was mental, not physical. I wasn't yet married. I ran into her one day. She said: 'You should get married.' I couldn't say anything. One or two years passed. I went to meet her. My feelings for her were now pure and chaste. I never had bad intentions towards her. I went into her garden after talking to her. I started searching for some fruit to eat but couldn't find anything.

A beautifully ripe guava was hanging from a branch. I couldn't climb trees, yet I climbed that one. I plucked the guava with great difficulty. There was only one. I climbed down. She had followed me into the garden. My body had got scraped a little in plucking that guava. I placed the fruit in her hands.

She said, 'Bhaiya, you have some?' I left without a word. I did not have the courage to say anything. My chest was bursting. I was diving into an ocean of joy. Indeed, the joy I felt then, I haven't felt since.

Eight–ten years had passed without my seeing her. One day I suddenly ran into her husband. I needed a clerk. I had advertised in the papers. Her husband had sent in an application—but didn't know that I was to be his officer. He said, 'I have submitted an application. If you can, please help me.' I had full authority to appoint candidates. I said, 'Don't worry. You will be appointed.' After a few days, his wife came to me. She asked to meet me. She fell at my feet and started crying: 'His job is in your hands. Please be kind.'

I soothed her. She had lost a lot of weight. Her terrible transformation deeply saddened me. I helped in her husband's advancement and made him head-clerk. I don't know where they are today. May god protect them.

Even today, every now and then, this memory from my adolescence turns my parched veins into the flowing Mandakini River. A strange wave surges in my heart. Those were days of such heavenly happiness! This scene ends, and the film of my wedding appears. The silent film of love turns into a talkie. This scene is also so pleasant and beautiful! A newlywed wife's love is so sweet and intoxicating. No one exists apart from the other. Being separated is so horrible. The first chapter of domestic life is so delightful! A new happiness flows through life. A person drowns in contentment. Could I ever forget the artful ways of my young wife? That map is engraved on my heart in a permanent glow. I was studying for my BA then. My father-in-law was worried about finding a groom for his daughter. Parents are never at peace until their young daughter is married off. One day, my father-in-law asked me, 'Do you have a good man in mind for her?'

I was just stepping into youth. I joked, 'Who can be better than me?' I caught his attention. Finally, after many efforts, he made me his son-in-law.

I got married. When I touched my wife's head for the first time, while applying sindoor, the only thought filling my heart was that she is now mine. I was happy. Just as I placed my hand full of sindoor on her forehead, it started drizzling. People said, 'The gods are blessing the bride and groom.'

I was appointed to a senior position after my BA. I spent twenty years of my life in great happiness. I used to get Rs 500 a month. My wife was faithful and gentle. I don't particularly remember any one incident from those times but the memory of Ramesh, oh! it makes my heart writhe. His tall, strapping, fair body, high forehead and broad chest drew all eyes—so why won't his memory agonize this unlucky wretch! Ramesh was my son. He wasn't fit to survive this sin-filled world, so the gods called him to them. The Almighty snatched away my twenty-three-year-old son. His future had been so bright. He was never second at anything. He passed his BA (English hon.) and MA with a first class. He went to England for the ICS. After his exams, he wrote to me saying he would return to India after travelling through Europe. He had begun his journey back home. His mother was enthusiastically awaiting his return. One day, a letter arrived, it seemed to have been written by Ramesh. When I opened it, my body turned to wood. Ramesh had written from the ship—

Respected Father and Mother—

I had great desire in my heart to see you but god didn't want this to happen. I am breathing my last. Please forgive my sins. Mother! This was God's will, no one can do anything.

Your beloved son,

Ramesh

There was another letter in the same envelope. The ship's Captain had written: Ramesh passed away soon after writing this letter.

I was reading this heartbreaking letter when the telegraph messenger arrived with a telegram. It said: 'Congratulations Ramesh, you have got the first position in the ICS.' I couldn't stand after reading those letters. I fell to the floor, unconscious. After this, Ramesh's mother went somewhat mad and even my mind turned unstable. One day, I slipped up in office and had to tender my resignation. Ramesh's mother is now better. I left the bungalow and rented a small room on the outskirts of the city where we have been living for the past ten years. There is no money. Whatever I earned, I spent on the poor. I was addicted to writing when I was young. My wife sends my old pieces to magazines. We have to make do with whatever we get for them. My wife is deeply affected by her son's death. Her heart is broken. Ah! how well I remember—a year after our wedding, my wife came up to me, cradling someone's child in her arms, and said, 'Wouldn't it be lovely if I had such a beautiful child!' Her words still strike my chest like lightning. The Almighty gave her a perfect child only to snatch him away. I remember one more thing as I lie dying. We have two brothers-in-law, both very successful. The younger is a judge in the high court. I can't even say it. Do poor people have judges as brothers-in-law? The other is the Additional Superintendent of Police. I remember one incident very well. My wife had said, 'Avadhesh is going to have a son. Please go and call on him.' I, a poor man, hesitated to go. Yet, I entered Judge Sahib's mansion.

There was a party of important people in progress. Many Englishmen were also present. Avadhesh was sitting with them. He saw me enter and lowered his head. Mr Justice Stout said, 'Who is this nasty old fellow in rags?'

Justice Sinha said, 'Might be some beggar.' Then he said, 'Go. Come back another day.'

I left, embarrassed. When I came outside, I learnt that Judge sahib had had a son and the party was being held in celebration. I was leaving when someone from the mansion called out, 'Aji oh miyan . . . please come inside.'

I turned and saw that Judge Sahib's wife was standing at the gate, calling me. I said, 'Sahib has asked me to come another day. I am leaving now.' I started walking away when the maid came up to me and said, 'Memsahib is calling you.'

I said, 'I am helpless' and turned to look at memsahib. Her eyes bore signs of helplessness. At home, I narrated everything to my wife. She was hurt by her younger brother's conduct.

My husband was narrating all of the above while lying with his head in my lap, and I was writing it down. Whenever he has to write something for a magazine, he keeps talking like this and I keep writing. After saying all this, he became restless. He said, 'Darling! The moment of my death is near. Now I have to say something to you. I am leaving but I am concerned about your future. How will you live all alone in this world? Go live with your brother. Dearest, I have scanned through all the events of my life. I haven't done anything bad. I remained untainted. This makes me happy. I am ready to embrace death, it's just my concern for you that troubles me. You have looked after me for forty-five years. Without you, I would have died long ago—only your care has kept me alive so long. Darling! When I was in college, one of my friends used to say that there is no such thing as pure or selfless love in this world. We would keep arguing, and neither of us would accept defeat. The love you have shown me bears not even the faintest hint of selfishness. In this Kaliyug, I have not seen another woman as faithful as you. I feel fortunate to have had you as my wife. You are truly a cursed goddess. It saddens me to leave you, but I have no choice. I have brought you a lot of grief. Forgive me, goddess!'

My husband kept speaking, and the tears kept flowing from my eyes. After all, could there be a woman so cold-hearted as to be unmoved at a time like this? The sun of my fortune was setting. My beloved husband, dearer to me than life itself, was leaving me. My auspicious sindoor was being erased. The steersman of my life-boat was leaving—how could I be at peace? I was sobbing. At that moment, I saw my policeman brother coming towards us. Avadhesh's son was with him. They entered the room and touched my feet. I couldn't contain myself and broke down, weeping.

I said, 'Bhaiya Ganesh, you have come after such a long time! My sindoor is being erased, please save my sinking boat somehow.'

Ganesh looked at my husband and asked, 'Bhai sahib, how are you?'

My husband smiled, 'Ganesh! I have met you at the moment of my death, this makes me happy. This is my last hour. It's futile to call a doctor. Tell me, have you come alone or with the family?'

Ganesh: 'With the family. Elder sister has also come with me.'

Husband: 'That makes me happy. Can you bring elder sister here? The sight of her would bring me much pleasure. Don't bring the boys. They will just make a pointless fuss.' (Looking at Avadhesh's son) 'Jagat, son, you go home, you have my blessing. May the Highest Soul keep you happy. Go and tell your mother and aunt that uncle remembered them at his hour of death. Send your older aunt here quickly. Go on, what are you waiting for?'

Jagat left, crying. A child's heart is so tender—who understands this? After some time, my elder sister came in. She became rather frightened at hearing all this. She stood at my husband's bedside. He extended his hands, touched the dust of her feet to his forehead and said, 'Didiji, I must have done some good deeds, since I got a chance to meet you. I didn't expect it. Just look after her.'

Sister: 'Why are you saying this? You will get better soon.'

Husband: 'That is a meaningless consolation. My survival is impossible.'

'Where is Ganesh?'

Ganesh: 'I am here.'

Husband: 'Bhaiya Ganesh, I am leaving. I just have one request—I have hurt you, forgive me. Please look after your sister. You are the sole support of this unfortunate woman. I don't understand why all of you are upset with me. Whatever it is, forgive me. What is the point of enmity with someone going into the lap of death? Eh! You are crying. Why are you being a coward—have patience.'

Ganesh: 'I am a sinner. It's due to my neglect that you are in this state. I don't deserve your forgiveness. Tell me, can a person who doesn't ask after his own kin even be called a human?'

Husband: 'No, Ganesh. These are all the fruits of karma. Even if you did make a mistake, the fire of your regret has engulfed it.'

I was standing next to Ganesh. As soon as my husband's eyes fell on me, he said, 'Sudha! I cannot remain unmoved at the sight of you. The dams of my heart break. Without me, you will be nothing but an uprooted vine. Let it be, what's the point of being so worried at the time of death? I have no words to bring you peace. I'm going now. (With folded hands) I hope that all of you will forgive me.' He paid his respects to everyone and closed his eyes. Then two hiccups, and his life-force flew away. I collapsed on his dead body, unconscious. I couldn't think straight. Now when I think of it, I remember one thing. He used to often recite a couplet—

Two hiccups decided the course of illness
One was death, one was your memory

Perhaps for my husband too, 'one was death, one was your memory'.

I was granted a godlike husband. I hope that I can serve him in my next life as well. It has been a year since his death. He said, 'Get my last pieces published in a magazine.' In accordance with his wishes, I am sending this article. After my husband's death, I did live with my brother but my heart wasn't at peace. A woman's place is in her husband's house. I returned to my sacred place after a few days. To the same little room where I spent ten unhappy years. I have decided to spend my last days here. I now live like an ascetic and spend my time in worship of my husband. I don't want to live in this world much longer. When god has left, there is no reason for the priest to linger.

ALAS, THE HUMAN HEART!

That little incident now doesn't seem as sharp and intense in memory's blurred and sombre shadow. Today, when I want to run away from this world of light, laughter and virtue to that ugly darkness in which I want to open my eyes with ebullience and insanity, I feel stifled. 'Today' means my success, my courage; and the failure and cowardice of those innumerable men and women who competed against me in the race of life. At least that's the conclusion I reach when I analyse myself consciously. It is beyond my ability to examine whether this is the truth or not. Society respects me for having submitted unequivocally to its restrictions and pettiness. But once— yes, my heart trembles in saying this at the peak of my success—my soul had rebelled against society. However, now that's just a story.

It was twenty years ago. I was staying at a small hill-station with a few of my doctor friends. We were all optimistic young men of similar age and carefree disposition. Days and nights were spent laughing, playing cards and hiking. No one had yet stopped to look life in the eye. One evening, when we were busy playing round after round of cards, the curtain rose on this tragic story. One of my playful friends saw her enter through the gates and said: 'Look, the queen of diamonds is finally here.'

And that is how, with a careless and cruel joke, we welcomed her, she whose eyes bore the poignant pain of the whole world.

She wasn't very old but time had not treated her gently. Her eyes were sunken, her lips were cracked, trying to contain a flood of emotions, like weak dams, in vain. She looked at us with her deep, bottomless eyes and said, 'Doctor sahib?'

I felt as if an arrow had pierced my heart, and was immediately overcome with remorse.

She came closer and said, 'My husband has a heart problem. I have arranged for conveyance, doctor sahib . . .' Neither could she say any more, nor was I waiting to listen to another word. I stood up, quickly put on my overcoat, stuffed all the essential equipment into my pockets and followed her out. My friends must have thought I was mad, eccentric, who knows, but offering myself to that unknown woman made me feel a kind of masculine victory and pride. At some distance, a handsome youngster was waiting with two horses. He bowed in greeting. We mounted the horses and galloped swiftly down the path of darkness. The difficulties of the route didn't allow me to think much about this brief novel. And yet, the plots of many unpleasant detective stories swirled in my mind. It felt as if I was stuck in a fatal but simple trap. Occasionally, the woman on my left, sitting on the horse with that beautiful man, seemed illusory.

When I saw some fireflies glowing at a distance, behind a cluster of pine trees, I shone my torch at my watch. It was nine o'clock. After three hours, I found myself back in the solid world of reality.

We had reached a small village, and now left the horses. That woman and I stood like spectres in front of a small stone house. She clanked the door chain and someone answered in a deep, dreamy voice. After five minutes, a young woman draped from head to toe in some faded colour, opened the door. By the dim light of her lantern, I noticed that she was staring at me with distrust and doubt. I turned to look at the woman who had brought me there but she was nowhere to be found. I looked in every direction, full of fear and uncertainty, but it was as if she had been swallowed by the sombre soul of darkness. Standing there at the door, I narrated my strange and impossible tale to the young woman and asked her, 'Is someone ill in your house?'

'There is no patient here,' she replied slightly sternly, 'but you can come in and meet my father. He is lonely and bitter—but he has no other ailment.'

The house was small. Only three rooms and a kitchen. Everything was lying around haphazardly. Broken furniture, chinaware, swamp-deer hides, everything strewn around carelessly. In one of the rooms, a middle aged man lay on a charpoy. The books and cigar butts all around him appeared strangely attractive to a visitor. Just one look at his dull, sallow face, and I could tell he was sick and that the ailment was serious. In the blink of an eye, I finally understood the whole affair. For some reason, the woman, this man's well-wisher, could not reveal herself. Upon receiving my introduction, the man bade me sit on a chair drowning in dust, and after listening to my story, uttered a blank and gloomy laugh. "It's crafted beautifully but no one's going to buy it here.' I asked him repeatedly to let me examine him, but he refused. He was a tough pessimist. He believed life to be a sin, a defeat, and said that a blind, cruel energy was running this polluted world. At the time, his words didn't hold much meaning to me—I thought they were a symptom of his illness. The girl brought me a cup of hot milk and some sweets, and I couldn't refuse her simple plea nor the man's request. After dinner, I lit a cigar and again requested the man to consider medical treatment. Seeing my sincerity, he finally agreed to an examination the next morning.

After the end of the night worship in the distant temple of the goddess, I came to the village hotel to spend the night. It was the town barber's house—he gave out some of the rooms on rent. I changed my clothes, sat in front of the fire in my room and had just begun to distractedly go over the evening's events when I heard someone's desperate voice outside. I thought: Let's see how the first night of the 100 nights of Alif Laila unfolds.

I came to the door and saw the girl, the second girl, holding a lamp, and staggering towards me. 'Yes?' I asked, both surprised and afraid.

'After you left, Father started coughing badly. He is quite critical now.'

I pulled on my overcoat and swiftly accompanied her. Behind us, there was a strange madness and agitation in the barking of the dogs that was disturbing my heart. When I got back to that house, I saw the man lying lifelessly on the charpoy. Beside him was a bent old servant, who had apparently just returned from somewhere and was now weeping. I examined the dead man and observed that, due to some sudden distress, his heart had failed. The girl understood immediately and, devastated, slumped on the broken table nearby. The old servant helped her up, and covered the dead body with a blue sheet.

After washing my hands, I suddenly noticed a large oil painting of a beautiful young woman hung near the corpse's bedside. 'This is the woman,' I screamed, 'the one who brought me here.'

The girl as if fell from the sky, and looked at me with distrust and fear: 'That is my mother, but she died 17 years ago, one year after my birth.'

At this, I should have been in an indescribable state but I wasn't, because the old servant dragged me outside by the arm. And the gist of what he told me , in a choked and trembling voice, is this: her husband had been serving in the army for a long time. When he finally returned, he found his wife was in madly in love with a young and handsome sarangi-player. After some time, she eloped with that man, leaving behind her one-year-old girl. Only a few days ago they had learnt that she was turning tricks in a nearby town.

Beloved readers, this story is over, make what you will of it, learn what you want from it. I just remembered someone's line— 'Alas, the human heart!'

AUNTY

In the course of human life, a stage arrives when even change is conquered. When the rise and fall of our life doesn't mean anything to us, and neither does it interest others. When we live only to remain alive, and death arrives yet doesn't.

Bibbo was at that stage of her life. The neighbours had always known her as an old woman, as if she'd originated old in the womb of eternity and turned immortal for a never-ending, unthinkable period. So as to not hurt her, young women would pretend to believe her imaginary stories. It was a matter of speculation whether she had anyone in this vast world. Most people believed that she was as alone as the creator of the cosmos. But she too had been a young woman once, even her eyes had once held nectar and poison. Even the withered tree facing the mercy of the storm had once cleaved through the earth's heart, swayed during spring and lived the solitary life of early winter. But Bibbo herself had forgotten all that. When we erase our innumerable sad memories, our happy memories are erased as well. But, what she had not forgotten was her nephew, her sister's son—Vasant. Even now, after she'd fed the cows, when she sat in the corner of her mud hut, in the light or shadow cast by her gourd-pumpkin creepers, his face would appear before her.

Vasant's mother had died only two months after his birth, and thirty-five years ago, his father had, with a pale, wan face, brought this news to Bibbo and then stood quietly before her with Vasant … she couldn't even dream of the things that happened after. If a leper hides his illness from others, he himself cannot look at it either—the life after was her diseased limb.

Vasant's father began to live there. He was younger than Bibbo. Bibbo, lonely Bibbo, thought: What's the harm? But then he left, and so, one day, only she and Vasant remained. Vasant's father was a part of the majority who lives only for dissatisfaction, who cannot bear the weight of contentment. She nurtured Vasant on the blood of her heart, but he flew away too as soon as he grew wings and once again she was all alone. She would hear of him sometimes. Ten years ago he came one day, wearing the black uniform of the Railways, and invited her to his wedding. Then she heard he'd left that job due to some indictment and set up business somewhere. Bibbo used to say that she was not at all interested in such matters. If Vasant were crowned king today she would not be pleased, and if he were hanged to death tomorrow she would not be sad. And she protested vehemently when her neighbours tried for some financial assistance from her nephew for her, the old aunt who made a living selling milk.

It was 2 p.m. Both of Bibbo's buckets were now empty. After putting the remaining milk to simmer, she was about to go for a bath when a middle-aged man holding a five-year-old boy by the finger walked into her courtyard.

'Can't help you now, 2 p.m. . . . ' Bibbo said, swift and terse.

'No, aunty . . .'

Bibbo went up to him, stared at him and then dreamily said, 'Vasant!' Then fell silent again.

'Aunty,' he said, 'I have no one in this world except you. My son is now motherless. You raised me—please raise him too. I will bear all the expense.'

'I've had enough, enough,' the old woman said shakily.

Bibbo was surprised to see that Vasant was growing old and that his son was just like Vasant and his father . . .

'Go away, Vasant,' she said, her voice hard. 'I can't do anything.' But Vasant kept pleading. He opened a small trunk and began to pull out presents for his aunt.

The old woman, pruning the unripened bottle gourds, kept asking Vasant to leave but there was unrest in her soul. She began to feel as if she were young again, as if Vasant's father, in the silence of the night, was kissing her a little in a dream . . . She drew Vasant close to her and began to sob.

Ho . . . but she would not look at Vasant's son. It was certain she would never keep him. Vasant felt hopeless. But, the next morning, when he went to wake Mannu, Bibbo snatched him away and held the little boy close. Vasant departed, leaving behind Mannu and a ten-rupee note.

Bibbo's milk wasn't selling any more. Three cows were sold off, one after another. Only Mannu's calf remained. Even the bottle-gourd and pumpkin customers were disappointed. Mannu—sallow, dull, lazy Mannu—was growing pink, quick and naughty. Disinterested Bibbo slowly let herself be entirely wrapped up in the boy and her household.

Vasant would send a money-order of five rupees each month, but within a year Bibbo had to mortgage her house. It had become necessary—to fulfil all of Mannu's wishes. Bibbo once again began to keep pace with time. People began to gossip and criticize her in the neighbourhood again. Mannu had re-established her bond with the society.

Then, one evening, Vasant suddenly returned. A short, wheatish woman was with him. She touched Bibbo's feet and said, 'Aunty, give Mannu to me, I will forever be grateful.'

'Yes,' said Vasant, with a despairing expression, 'it's better than jeopardizing someone's life . . . If I had known, why would I have got married?'

'Okay,' said Bibbo, 'take him.'

Mannu was playing in the house next door. The old woman clambered onto the wall with trembling limbs and called him.

He dashed home hopping and skipping. The new mother hugged him to her bosom. The child couldn't understand a thing—he ran to the old aunt.

'Go, go away.' Bibbo admonished.

The poor child was unable to understand the meaning of this admonishment. He began to cry.

Vasant stood there, astonished. Bibbo grabbed Mannu's hand, washed his face, and, taking down his shoes from the courtyard ledge, helped him put them on.

Vasant's wife smiled, 'Aunt, won't you let us stay for a day? What's the hurry?' But Bibbo had as if entered a different realm. One where no sound of this world could reach. In the blink of an eye, she packed up all Mannu's things, things given in love and play. She told Mannu he was going on a trip with his new mother.

Mannu ran to his father. Bibbo brought over a few notes: 'Keep your money.'

Vasant was in a dilemma but his wife resolved it. She picked up the notes. 'Aunt, we don't have enough right now but will send more as soon as we return. We will never be able to repay our debt to you.'

Mannu wasn't happy for long at his parents'. He fell ill twice a month. His new mother wasn't too happy to have him either. Finally, after lying awake all night and despite his wife's protests, Vasant once more left with Mannu for his aunt's.

When he reached, he saw a crowd before her frail door. The neighbours surrounded Vasant as soon as they saw him: 'She's your aunt. Her door's been shut for five days. We're worried!'

Breaking the door open, they saw the old woman lying on the earth, clutching a photograph. As if by dying, she was providing proof of being human.

Except for Vasant, no one knew that the picture was his father's. And even he couldn't understand why it was there!

FREEDOM: A LETTER

That same month of March has returned. Today may even be the same date. But I am not writing to you for such a petty reason. In reality, my dear friend, in the past year something has 'happened' to me about which I am writing to you today after delaying it many times; I feel I should have written long ago. In the meantime, by remaining silent for this past year, you have shown a wisdom that only we, who have gone through so much, can understand.

That student, the one who that evening said such sweet-and-sour things à la Isadora Duncan, suddenly died last September. A few days before she left the hostel, she placed a nagfani plant on her windowsill and, god knows whether in jest or due to some deep pathetic disorder, began to worship it just like our ancestors. Then one day she went back home after falling slightly ill, and a month later, in the morning, we spotted a man resembling a whimsical cowboy-movie character coming out of her room behind the housemaid. It was her father, come to collect her things. And so, that is how our little Isadora Duncan died, and I think no other death would have been quite as appropriate for her. Don't you feel that we neither live our own lives nor die our own deaths? The charity hospital-gown-like life neither looks good nor fits well, and, even if it is clean and washed, death inhabits it like the stench of chloroform. Often I feel that our greatest tragedy is not that we don't live our own lives but that we don't die our own deaths. Because it is only death that gives meaning to our life's pettiness, to a pile of unrelated and pointless events. I am sure that you will call this the 'logic of sophistry'. I remember you said that in matter nothing is either born or destroyed. Man himself has created birth and death so that it may elevate himself with these poetics.

Yes, Bhuvan, let me take a break from this discussion and tell you about the event, because if I don't tell you now, I will not be able to tell you in the whole letter. I am the mother of one-two-month-old child.

It all happened so simply and suddenly that, at first, I couldn't even accept it myself. I used to stay up nights naively thinking about it. It was the end of term, and a month-long holiday from hospital duties was about to begin. Yes, I used to constantly think about this new *phenomena* and, right from the beginning, refused to be even a little bit scared. It was only when I was going home that the fear began—a strange, blurred fear but one which caused no pain, merely irritation and exhaustion. All through the train ride, I experienced strange turns. I wanted to, but could not tell what other people thought of me. The night of the journey was very troublesome. I started talking to other people to distract myself but they evaded me with half-hearted responses. What had happened to me! I was experiencing something strange. Believe me, how often I wanted to lament and weep loudly or yell: O! you children of the Devil! When I finally fell asleep, I kept dreaming of that withered, dust-ridden nagfani plant. In the morning, at Kathgodam, I felt better. You know how magical Kathgodam's damp air and blue—completely blue—hills appear, especially after a whole night's journey. I travelled comfortably in a lorry till Almora. Something was growing inside me, and I felt that I could tell my mother everything. My courage grew as I reached the Almora crossing. Then I saw the new pastor's wife, Mrs Nabi, smiling crudely as she shook her umbrella at me. At first, I wanted to laugh but then realized that when she got to know, she would give me that same vulgar, sheepish smile, and then mumble something meaningless before walking away quickly, swinging her umbrella . . . and then . . . and then . . .

Ma was alert as soon as she saw me. She tried to feign normalcy but the burden was too much for me. I burst out, 'Mama, I can return to my job only after a year.' Mama looked at me painfully for a moment, then slowly walked into the inner room. Then, from behind the curtain, she said, 'Do whatever you want but I swear on God, on the Cross, not in front of me.'

I suddenly remembered that she had once said the same thing in that same voice and tone. My heart sank. The striped yellow, wrinkled curtains fluttered like fluid fire.

One day, during our childhood, my eldest brother Tim decided to keep a pet bitch. Both her hind legs were damaged, and she could only drag herself around. Maybe that's why some Bhotiya had abandoned her. Tim began to pet her as soon as he saw her and named her Gypsy. Mama laughed a lot at the name but refused to let her in the house. So Tim and I built her a house of jute sacking under Rawat Sahib's bungalow. One day, Tim came and gasped that Gypsy had given birth to one, two, three, four children! And Mama, from behind the curtain, had said, just like today, 'Do whatever you want but I swear on God, on the Cross, not in front of me.'

Tim and I wrapped those mice-like little pups in jute and drowned them in Narayan Tiwari's pond. They kept floating back up until Tim finally beat them down with a stick. That day, Tim kept running through the house, biting his own hand . . .

I couldn't stay here. My own mother had turned against me.

The hostel was empty for the holidays, only a couple of final-year girls had stayed back. I left my luggage there, then went straight to the hospital and told Sarupi everything. At first, Sarupi didn't believe me but then, when she finally did, she ran upstairs, shouting something like 'Gladys' baby!' and dragged the new house surgeon down—she was mad with happiness and excitement. The house surgeon bemused; he said, 'Baby? What baby?' and Sarupi, laughing, pushed him out of the room.

But who is the man?

It is fine that we would not like to punish him. The entire burden of the punishment must be borne by you (i.e. the woman). At most, we can sentence you to spend your life with that treacherous, unprincipled man. This is why it is not just the duty but also the great moral and social responsibility of the woman to reveal the name of her seducer. However, I am respectably unemployed, a significant economic unit, and that is why, instead of standing in the witness box, I am sitting on the judges' bench. It's a small town, here everyone believes that 'Doctorni Madam' is raising some orphan child. But there is something more.

Some time last winter, I was on night duty in the hospital. One morning, as I was walking from one ward to another, I saw him in the distance. I immediately recognized his serious and somewhat conceited walk, and his bird's nest-like hair. The demeanor of poets is rather common among doctors. He spotted me too, and paused as he walked past me. He mentioned he was being commissioned for the war effort but wanted to open his own clinic. After making some more small talk, he left.

The second time, he came by with Sarupi one evening in Nainital. The child was in the crib and I was staying with Sarupi. My job was still uncertain, but I was mentally and physically well. At the sight of him, I suddenly started laughing. Obviously, he had heard about the child but was feigning ignorance, so neither Sarupi nor I mentioned the child. He talked about his life's difficulties and disappointments with me for the first time, and said that he might have no option but to join the army. And now his letter is in front of me where he has written that he will be sailing from Bombay on the 8th, that is today, perhaps without knowing that his child has totally fulfilled the heart and life of a woman. I had decided from the start that I would not tell him, I didn't want him to feel obligated, and I couldn't bear the idea that a man as helpless and pathetic as him should pity me. Truth be told, this child means nothing to him. And for me, it is a truth that I have felt through the suffering of my body and soul. It has created an unexpected strength, joy, and longing for freedom in me.

What is this thing called freedom? Nothing can be known about it without acquiring and using it.

IN THE WOMB OF THE FUTURE

It was dusk. Sunlight was fading after burning bright all day. It was making preparations to depart. A chorus of birds was singing auspicious songs on the occasion. And yet, the wind kept blowing sombrely. At times like this, a happy person grows happier and a sad person sadder. In the garden, Louisa was sitting in a meditative state on a large stone before her father's grave. One feeling after another kept surging like ocean waves in her heart. Suddenly someone called out: 'Louisa!' Louisa's chain of thought was broken. She looked at the visitor with tearful eyes and, after an instant, hid her face between her knees.

Charles came up to Louisa. He put a hand on her shoulder and said, 'Louisa, it's been fifteen days since your father died and you're still crying like a silly child. Be grateful to the Almighty that your father remained victorious till the end. He served his motherland (Spain) all his life. Even at the end, despite a fierce revolution, ethical-unethical, a ferocious struggle between fascism and democracy, he brought you from an unsuitable place to a safe one. You tell me: Did a single wish of his remain unfulfilled? You should be proud of your courageous father's valiant death. You must remember how, at the time of his death, a radiant peace and contentment was playing on his face. Get up now, Louisa, wash your face and hands, and see how nature's silent call is being expressed in the twittering of birds.' Who knows if Louisa, her head bent, was listening to all this or thinking about something else. After Charles stopped speaking, Louisa looked up at him with tearful eyes and said timidly, 'Charles'. Her voice held a tremor, her tone distress and her face the faint sign of a confused wish.

Charles felt a chill. Oh! The tears of a beloved hold microbes of the destruction of innumerable towering summits, the applause of innumerable devastating meteor showers and the spark of endless gruesome fires. It was only to be expected that poor Charles would tremble.

Charles realized that Louisa was nursing a sorrow other than her father's death, which she hadn't been able to share. Her stifled voice made his heart even heavier. He was in love with Louisa. He couldn't bear to see her suffer. If he couldn't make Louisa happy, his life would be meaningless. Passionately but resolutely, he said, 'Louisa, tell me, what else is bothering you? I promise that as long as I am alive, I will try to solve every one of your problems.' Charles' eyes were shining. Such great commitments are made but once in a lifetime. The rest of one's life is spent in fulfilling them.

Louisa listened to Charles' promise. A strange mixture of hope and happiness, awe and peace, fear and melancholy played across her face. But how could she suddenly utter what she had been trying in vain to say for a week? Charles loved her. But Louisa did not want Charles. Her heart was longing for Philips who was detained in Spain to fight with the nationalist army against the anarchists. She wanted Charles to bring her news of him.

Louisa's silence made Charles impatient. Forcefully, he said again, 'Tell me, Louisa, what is that thing whose lack you continuously feel? What is that sorrow that has been disturbing you these past many days? Just name it, and see what Charles can do.'

Louisa couldn't contain herself. She gathered what fragments of courage she possessed and said, 'Charles, my companion from Spain, Philips Madrid, has been detained in Spain to fight against the anarchists. I haven't heard from him since then. God forbid he ...' She couldn't say any more. She buried her face in her hands and started sobbing.

Charles finally understood Louisa's state. He was stunned. His surging heart had felt that should Louisa ask for the stars in heaven, he would fetch them by drilling a hole in the sky; that should she ask for a lofty memorial on her father's grave, he would build at once a towering monument; that should she have a problem with some senior official, he would behead him in an instant. But the cobra hadn't foreseen the demand for its own gem. The creature had never imagined it would be asked for its own life. His face darkened and his head drooped. Yet, he said softly, 'All right, Louisa, I will find out about your Philips at once.'

Louisa looked up at him, distraught.

It was dawn in the Carcasonne region of France. The cruel rays of Helios had attacked the earth after slaughtering the stars. The face of the firmament was red with anger. But it grew calmer upon seeing its unchallenged dominance spread through the atmosphere.

Who could tell when the flame of revenge flickering in its depths would flare up into a blaze?

Charles was preparing to leave. After donning his clothes, he took up his weapons and went out of the house. The horse was ready. He was about to leap upon it when Louisa rushed out and said, 'Wait a few minutes, Charles, I'm coming with you.' Charles, taking the reins in his hands, said, 'No, Louisa, no, you have no idea of the condition of Spain today. No one bothers about anyone else. Every hour, heavy bombs rain down from the sky. Don't be foolish. I will find out about Philips and, if possible, bring him back with me. You wait here.' Louisa wanted to stop him but by the time Charles finished speaking, his horse was already far away. She was silent. But she knew what she had to do.

The Pyrenees mountain range, knotted like strings, ran from east to west. Nature had gifted this wall as an offering of peace for the constant political struggles of Spain and France—it had tried to keep the two countries separated by means of this colossal comma. However, humans had used the strength of science to disregard nature and establish their links. Trains—indicators of human power—ran between north and west Pyrenees squealing with victorious pride at nature's defeat. But the native inhabitants of the hills, too poor to live on humanity's ruthless base, had to resort to the shelter of the loving lap of nature. They had discovered a straight but rough path for crossing the Pyrenees. It could be crossed easily on foot or on the back of a mule. Humans don't like delay in times of mental turmoil. So Charles had taken this route. Foolish Louisa now followed him.

The route was unfamiliar and dangerous. And the horse was large. Louisa encountered difficulties at every step. At every moment, she was scared of falling. But the horse kept galloping on. She used to ride with Papa but never along such dangerous paths or under such horrible circumstances. She was feeling the pressure in her knees. Every limb was aching. But she wouldn't stop. She kept moving in a straight line. On, Louisa, on! The test of love is arduous.

Suddenly she realized that the border of Spain was near. Border guards were bound to be present. If someone were to stop her—well, she would see. She has a pistol, after all. She tucked it in more securely. The horse was flying on and her impassioned heart was roaming the dark womb of the future. 'Charles must have reached Spain by now. His life is in danger. An hour ago, he said heavy bombs rain down from the sky. If one of them—' Her heart quickened in time with her flickering eyes. Imagination ran wild on the path of emotion. 'Charles has placed his life in danger because of me. Such a brave, noble, resolute man is pointlessly at risk because of me. I am so unfortunate. Oh god—' her heart shivered with dread. Charles . . . now inhabited it. Sympathy had turned into love. The horse was rushing down a slope. At that moment, she had no idea of direction, place, etc. Suddenly someone shouted. 'STOP!' Startled she saw many Spanish soldiers lined up nearby. The 'STOP' order had come from one of them. She dismounted, took her pistol. She walked towards the soldiers. She wanted to ask them about Charles, too. All of a sudden, she noticed Charles' familiar horse tied up on her left. Her entire gaze turned towards it. A body was lying next to the horse, covered with white cloth. Her heart shuddered. She shivered with the same dread she had felt before.

Taking quick, long strides, she reached the corpse. She removed the cloth. It was as though she was paralysed. Betrayed, she stood there for a moment. A scream escaped her lips and then she turned speechless. It was Charles.

A few sprinkles of water returned Louisa to consciousness. She was just getting up when someone called out, 'Louisa!' The voice was familiar. She started. She turned and saw Philips, in military uniform. She asked in a tender, questioning tone, 'Philips?'

'Yes, Louisa,' Philips answered. Her eyes turned to Charles' corpse again. His face, despite being lifeless, was still deeply flushed, due to the intensity of his feelings. Signs of peace and victory were clearly visible on his bloodless face. His huge, open eyes were as though testifying to the horrifying promise as well as its horrifying fulfilment. Louisa felt distraught. In a serious tone, she asked, 'Do you know anything about Charles' murder, Philips?' 'Yes, Louisa,' Philips answered, surprised, 'Charles, who? No one can enter here without proper papers. I was obligated by law to punish him. But what does it have to do with you? Where is your father? Where are you coming from?'

She didn't seem to hear the last few questions. In a trembling but astonished voice, she said, 'You are Charles' murderer, Philips?' Philips was taken aback. Louisa, too, was bewildered. Philips—dearer to her than life itself, was standing before her eyes and she couldn't even utter two words of love. What a strange situation. On the one hand, union, on the other, eternal separation. The clash of feelings had driven Louisa mad. Like one deranged, she stood up. She went and kissed Charles' horse. The horse whinnied but the next moment, its head drooped as though in disappointment at the failure to fulfil a past pledge. Leaving the horse behind, Louisa started walking aimlessly down the path to nowhere. Philips was crying out, 'Louisa, Louisa!' But she kept on walking—towards endlessness, beyond the horizon—where the voice of Louisa's inner self was calling, 'Charles! Charles!'

MASTERNI

That day it had been raining from the morning. By dusk, the hill village seemed to be drowned in a boundless yellow fog. Hidden, deserted streets, unsightly fields, monotonous little houses—everything had fused together in that yellow fog.

The women had shut their doors and were busy disentangling and sorting yarn. The men were in the next village. It had a missionary quarter and a furnace. Really, the slow, monotonous and soft splash of rain could not be heard there.

A few minutes before 4 p.m., the door of a cottage opened. This cottage was even smaller and meaner than the ordinary houses. Through its creaking wooden door, five-six girls and boys emerged, stooped like old farmers, trying to save their bags from the rain, silently walking down the curved streets before disappearing from sight. As long as they were visible, the masterni kept standing silent and straight, staring in their direction. Then, she went back in, closing the door firmly and defiantly.

She was a middle-aged Christian woman—difficult and serious. She had come to this Christian village two years ago, and, with the help of a Hindustani missionary, set up this school. In these two years, her face had grown even longer, even paler, even more irritable. Despite living in the village, she seemed apart from it. The women were scared of her, and the men looked at her with defiance.

Faced with the day's blue, blue hills and dense fog, she shivered and, every now and then, rubbed her body with her hands.

After this, the village was deserted once again. Just once the masterni opened her door, peered out, then quickly closed it.

At around 6 p.m., when the yellowness of the fog was turning blue with the hills, a human being was finally seen in the village. A tall, sickly sixteen or seventeen-year-old boy. Wearing an old military coat. His dirty shirt was visible outside the collar. To avoid the slush, he hopped like a frog from one side of the street to the other. He breathed a sigh of relief when he reached the termite-eaten wooden door and climbed the threshold after shaking himself like a wet dog.

'Sister Lucy,' he shouted, 'it's so dark!'

'Tutu!' the masterni shook her hands free and, moving slowly, lit the lantern that hung from the ceiling. Into that small, dark, filthy room, light began to flow like blood from the lamp.

In the meantime, Tutu was looking for a spot to hang his large, heavy coat while grumbling about the rain and the road.

'Listen, do you have a piece of cloth—a torn piece of blanket or something? I want to clean my shoes.'

The masterni bent down silently and cleaned his shoes. Tutu, looking down, kept repeating, 'No, no.'

The masterni, still bent over, asked, 'Is everyone well at home?'

'I have many letters for you. Only Murli is cross with you. Some stockings you knit for her! She's turning blue from the cold.'

He handed the letters to his sister, moved near the light and started running his fingers through his wet hair. Every now and then he'd mutter something. The masterni would raise her head from the letters to look at him and then resume reading.

Then, keeping the letters aside and turning her attention to the tall, smooth-cheeked sixteen-year-old boy before her, she began to think about him. She remembered him as a baby. Holding his warm-soft body against hers, she would feel like a ripened fruit.

'You're not reading the letters,' he said, turning suddenly.

'I've read them,' she said, and then began to pace up and down again, running her hands along her body. Her brother stared at her and, seeing that she had finished reading the letters, muttered, 'Murli's socks. And Mummy said . . .'

The Masterni's voice seemed to slice through like a knife: 'And how is Papa?'

Tutu made a funny face and said, 'The same.'

Papa, ill, abandoned, ignored—he never wrote to her, never asked anything of her.

'What do you do?'

'Me! I work every day with Father Tiwari. Mummy would kill me if I didn't. Mummy and Murli just waste their time.'

'You are a man,' his sister said as though in a dream, and started pacing again.

'I'll become a priest . . . in two years,' Tutu said with a mix of pride and bemusement.

They remained silent for some time. Then the masterni, sitting on a trunk, started knitting quickly. Every so often, a strange, bitter smile flickered on her pale, chapped lips.

Tutu felt anxious every time he looked around at the broken chairs and dirty pillows in that filthy room.

'What's this! Murli's stockings?' he blurted in a strange fear.

'Can't you see?' the masterni barked.

Since the moment he'd arrived, Tutu's heart was growing heavier, like a sodden blanket. He kept thinking about his sister, this house, as if he was looking at new constellations through a telescope.

The windows were turning blind. As if dirty, woolly clouds had occupied the earth.

Footsteps were heard at the door. Two little girls entered, holding hands. They were wearing short frocks of coarse cloth and their faces were sunburnt like peasants.

The older girl placed a dirty enamel plate on the bed. It was covered with a red cloth. Then she stood to one side, clutching her younger sister's hand.

'Do you want the plate?' The masterni asked without looking up. The two girls nodded in unison, and said, 'Yes'.

The masterni got up and removed four eggs, a few half-ripened tomatoes and a cheap brass brooch from the plate.

'Tell your father that Masterni said to, okay?' And she again ran her hands down her body.

The girls left as silently as they had come.

Tutu had watched them with a strange interest. After they left, he turned his face towards the window and asked, 'Sister Lucy, don't you drink tea?'

The masterni suddenly stopped in the middle of the room.

'Listen, here are five rupees, and here are Murli's stockings and this is Mummy's vanity box. Tell them never to ask me for anything ever again. Let them die, let them go to the church.'

Like a mad person, she mimed giving him the money, the stockings and the vanity box with her two small, wrinkled hands, and spoke as if her blood was freezing.

'I...I say let them go to the church, let them die in the mission.'

Tutu said painfully, 'Sister Lucy!'

Lucy softened a little and opened the north window of the room. As soon as the window opened, the light in the room fluttered like a caged bird.

'I have nothing—nothing,' she said, 'You can search the entire house,' and then closed the window with a bang.

Tutu was startled by the sound but couldn't utter a word.

The masterni sat down on her bed. Gripped its side with both hands. Suddenly she felt battered by all the wounds of her life, little and big. She had no more energy to think. A slow, knotted pain was flowing through her whole being. And now it wanted to ooze out and drown her.

Tutu said with a sudden harshness, 'Sister Lucy!'

But just then someone from outside said in a throaty voice, 'Teacher, may I come in?'

Tutu moved towards the voice. The masterni ran forward in disgust, opened the door slightly, went outside and closed it. Tutu only caught a glimpse of him. A middle-aged farmer with an extinguished face—like the ones who doffed their hats and begged in church on Sundays. In a minute the masterni was back. Her face harder than before. She looked at Tutu, turned away and muttered to herself, 'Why me? I have nothing to do with you . . . I ask you people …' She clasped her hands to her sides and started pacing up and down.

'It's as though I've been buried alive. At least let me have the peace of the grave.' she spread out her hands, begging.

Tutu sat glumly gazing at the light. Suddenly she grabbed his hand. 'Go, sleep.'

Tutu obeyed. But when he lay down, he turned his face towards the dirty, damp wall and began to weep. At first, faintly. Then, louder and louder.

The masterni kept pacing up and down. Then slumped onto the charpoy. Tutu finally stopped crying. Silence spread through the room.

Only sometimes from far, far away, the strange sounds of the night watchmen would shatter against the surrounding hills and fall, fall into this room.

MOTHER AND SONS

Everyone sitting around the charpoy breathed a deep sigh, in unison. All of them were exhausted, defeated. There was silence in the room, and even the dying person's breath was tired and defeated. For the past three days, they had all been watching the battle of death and waiting for its victory. The neighbours would come by whenever they could, whisper with drawn faces, 'What does the doctor say?' or something along those lines, then leave after offering an opinion or few words of advice at the sight of the dying person's snuffed out, empty face. They were all part of the revolving world. Only the dying person was gently, swiftly separating. The people around the charpoy were doing what has always been done at a time like this, and were prepared or preparing for what has always happened at such times. After all, the dying person was only their mother, grandmother, sister.

So the elder daughter Kuccho didn't come after getting her brother's two letters—her daughter was pregnant—but did finally come with her daughter as soon she got the telegram. The elder son does night duty in the Railways, who will cook his parathas in the morning, the younger son doesn't host games of flash any more, and how does this have anything to do with his mother's illness or death, sometimes she wants to know. The little one is still young, she's only been married three years. She used to tell tales about the younger sister-in-law to the older sister-in-law, and still does. What effect the mother's illness or death is having on them she doesn't know, she doesn't want to know. The oldest son is turning middle-aged, separated from the family, his wife has had a separate kitchen for seventeen years now, she has many complaints against the dying one. She wants to forget them today. Even if she agrees to pay half the medical bills and funeral expenses, she won't give the money to the younger one. Who wants to argue with her! Na, she won't get in the middle of all this. The younger daughter-in-law is desperate to complain for the fifth time that the elder daughter-in-law went to sleep early last night after lying about her child crying. She would have called the civil surgeon, but why is the eldest only screaming, 'Civil surgeon, civil surgeon'? Is everyone else here a yokel? Stupid?' The two sons have lived separately for so long that they feel strange being together today. Both look at the thermometer together, measure out the medication together. Both want to speak to the Ayurveda doctor . . . Apart from them, there are the children. Their parents gather them and say: 'Boys, girls! Grandmother is leaving us, see!' They whisper in the dying one's ears, 'Amma! Your grandsons are touching your feet, give them your blessings.' The dying person opens her eyes and mutters something. She alone is dying. She alone is being exploited. The life that has set and stabilized over seventy-five years of heat and cold and rain is once again falling apart.

The elder daughter says, 'Amma! What are you thinking? Look at us. Take God's name!'

The elder daughter-in-law says, 'Amma! Chant Rama's name. Be delivered of your sins.'

The younger one, covering her face in the presence of the older brother-in-law, takes a deep breath and says, 'Who could be as pure a soul as Amma?'

The elder son picked up the medicine bottle from the cornice. The younger son yawned and said, 'The yellow bottle has the topical ointment.' The elder son made a face, held Amma up and made her drink the medicine. After which, burying her face in the pillow, she turned towards the wall. Her tangled sparse white hair lay scattered across the dirty pillow.

The younger daughter-in-law wanted to change the bedding, but the elder one didn't think so. The younger one said again, 'Amma, what is that stain on your saree? Do you want to change?' Amma turned and stared at her. Everyone's faces were similar and plain. They were all filled with life. As though she was searching for something else in them. It is said that at the time of death, one's entire life passes like a film in front of one's eyes, the mind slows down and rests again and again only on events of the fixed—and fully formed—past. Perhaps she does or doesn't remember; but her mind was becoming like a vacuous, speechless animal. When she glimpsed their faces in the light of the old 'Dietz' lantern, she suddenly wondered: Why were they all such failures? Even before the elder son was born, she had wanted him to be a lawyer, like that other boy in the neighbourhood. But why didn't he become a lawyer? She turned towards him. He came close to her and asked, 'What is it, Amma?' She felt at peace with him for no reason. She asked for some water.

She lay down after drinking it, tired. People were talking around her. The elder daughter's pregnant daughter sat down beside her. Her mother wanted her to get up. The younger son was thinking about something, feeling sad. All at once, Amma called out faintly, 'Young one!' The younger son went up to her and shed some tears. Amma turned her face away. Drying his tears, he said, 'We'll fetch the big doctor in the morning' and went out of the room, wiping his nose with his dhoti. The elder daughter-in-law was feeding milk to the boy in her lap. She said with a knowledgeable air, 'Yes, call the civil surgeon, the big shot!' The younger daughter-in-law made a face. The young daughter caught on and smiled. The elder daughter bared her teeth and said, 'How much will he charge?'

The elder son said, 'Is the big doctor God Almighty?' And everyone fell silent. Amma heard everything and realized that the big doctor was not god. As soon as she thought of god, she realized that she was as far away from god as ever. Only now, there was an inconvenience and trouble in her that wasn't present before. She began to carefully notice every object in the room. She had seen these things a million times before, to the point that they had lost their real shape. But today every object appeared separate and sharp. She is angry with the elder daughter-in-law. Once she'd even said that she'd never drink water from her hands, even if she was dying! The younger daughter-in-law is good. She has cared for her; but today she is seeing both of them anew. She can see that both are poor, both are helpless. Why helpless? she began to wonder—

forgetting that she herself was helpless. Then she muttered, 'Kuccho! Kuccho!' The elder daughter got up, arranging her saree, but Amma's face had turned white as a stone.

The old woman looked at her very closely.

Elder daughter-in-law: 'Amma is deep in thought.'

Elder son: 'Worldly attractions and illusions surround her! The world is a bizarre spectacle.'

Elder daughter-in-law: 'Who knows what's written in one's destiny!' (Younger daughter-in-law, taking a deep breath, faintly) 'She must be thinking about Babuji!'

But Amma wasn't thinking about Babuji (her husband). All that was very far away. Her mind had no more energy to crawl towards it. She was moving far, far away from these people slowly, slowly.

These people were real failures. A person can fully understand another person's meaningless and pitiful failure only at the time of death. Kuccho had once been gorgeous and full of life. First-born, the darling of her parents. Married off ambitiously. But, defeated by time's warrior, she had turned vacant. Amma once loved her boundlessly, a love that eventually went to the elder son. He also remained unsuccessful. Amma had created patterns of deep colours for all of them but the patterns had all broken. Not one of them was close to her, not one was hers. At this moment, only that was hers which she herself had created. Maybe she had asked too much of them, but so what? Is it not enough to make someone your own?

At midnight, everyone was sleeping on mattresses on the floor, only Amma was awake and, as if, drowning. Wondrously, even her troubles were drowning. She started thinking of faraway things. Meaningless, unparalleled. Some house, some man once glimpsed somewhere, she started hearing strange sounds. But this state didn't last long. She started feeling nervous, as if she was frightened of being alone on a dark road. There was no energy in the body, she had known it for a while, she had grown used to it, but she was ready to fight for that energy now. Everyone was sleeping. She could hear their breaths, she recognized them, but what is all this to her when her body has no more energy? She will fight for it! Peace disappeared from her face. It was replaced with a bitter battle. Her face turned sharp and even more lifeless.

Fortunately, the elder son woke up from an unpleasant dream. He coughed, sipped the water at his bedside, and came up to Amma. He bent and looked at her face in the faint light. He wanted to wake up the younger sister sleeping with her head on the side of the bed, but then he caressed Amma's hair and said, 'Amma!' Amma looked at him, startled and felt as if her inner struggle quieted down. This gave her a little peace. The elder son again called out, 'Amma!' Amma once again woke as if from deep sleep. Her entire mind focused on her son. For an instant, she forgot everything except him. A deep and ardent desire flowed from her breasts. To give him something—something!—

'Do you want some water?' asked the son.

Each part of Amma's body wanted to answer but she couldn't say anything. The battle resumed. She turned her face and started breathing heavily.

The elder son, worried, placed his hands on her arms and said, 'What is it, Amma?'

Suddenly Amma found an old familiar flame enter her like arrows from all sides. She thought this flame had been extinguished forever; but right now, during this total and real battle, this mere touch made the ancient flame dance in her every pore. She shivered and the whole battle turned towards the flame. The elder son, holding his trembling mother strongly, drew her close. Their chests united, the flame became even stronger, and it moved from below the waist and started circling in her calves. She raised her weak hands with difficulty and started stroking his back with a ghost-like touch. The battle was over. Only her weak, dying hands, with an inner inspiration, kept rubbing the son's back, and then slowly ceased. The elder son had never seen someone die before, so he couldn't even wake the others in time.

If someone stops cooperating with 'today', 'tomorrow', 'now', 'when', 'then' and thinks 'what', is irritated by why this laughable Bali contained Time after swallowing-tolerating so much! Why was this card-house of 'past', 'future', 'present' erected; yes, if someone thinks 'what', is irritated that the present containing everything within it like a tortoise is so cold and hard, and then observes it, but why observe it only, why not pick a composition from Creation's huge, blind presence and dissolve it under a micro-scope; but why not observe only that! Yes, look at her—the woman's—body, her name and her security and get irritated.

But why get irritated? Why, after all? Is irritation the ultimate? Without it, would tragedy necessarily burst out into ugly laughter? It is true that, by the unchanging laws of science, like liquid she took the form of the mould of life—she loved one man, married another, broke one's heart, kissed his photograph, came too close to another and left him warped, and if someone were there to shed tears for her, he must have laughed.

'Prema,'—the broken-hearted one said in a choked voice—'love, this is not a game, it is . . .'

'I wish it were a game, believe me, I would have forgotten my defeat and congratulated you on your victory.' Her soul was as vacant and complete as an animal's.

The broken-hearted one said to Prema insistently, 'You will regret it, you . . .'

'I have done everything else, I will do this, too.'

Life's debt has to be repaid completely, her soul had the shallow boldness of a philosopher. And after this, she displayed her tears before hiding them. Instead of making a promise to him, she made him make promises. Used the word 'notoriety' three times despite knowing its meaning; however, all this was now covered in the dust of time. Now she was a resolute, incompletely complete, completely incomplete, affluent woman. She burnt Keshav's letters after making her husband read them, then laughed at her first fancy, and forced her husband to laugh as well. Hung his photograph in her bedroom, gathered up his gifts, carelessly threw them somewhere, and picked them up again, then after forgetting their extraordinariness, she breathed an air of astute relief as though her whole life, the good and the bad, was part of her like a female kangaroo's baby. All this has been scattered over the last five years like some irregular venture. Through these last five years, Keshav has been moving further and further away from her, there was no point in being close anyway. But after five years on this merry-go-round, they came face to face again and something strange, funny, fragile, disabled stood between them. Its tale is as follows:

Prema's husband is an officer in the Railways. Regularly travels outside headquarters for work, Prema sees him off at the station, he smiles at her, she at him. He wants to talk about something serious, she asks, 'Who is that? The one who has many dogs?' He presses her hand, she smiles, complains about her high heels, waves her handkerchief or umbrella nervously when the train leaves and sets off swiftly, thinking about something else. On one such night, she had brought along her two-year-old. As he was leaving, she tried to take the child but the child refused and she said, just like that, 'Take him with you, maybe he'll be content with his Papa.' And he really took the child with him. His peon was imitating the child's laugh with his toothless mouth and snapping his fingers. She, drowning, having forgotten herself, started running alongside the train, 'My baby.' The husband said with anxiety, irritation and fear, 'Behave!' She couldn't decide whether his tone was one of fear or admonishment. After pausing for a minute, she started walking back swiftly. And then she saw Keshav sitting on a holdall with his back against 'Hindu Water'. She paused nervously, then stood there smiling—but Keshav kept reading the timetable with total attention as if it was a poem by 'Nirala'. She smiled again. More dramatically. Keshav stood up and remained standing.

Prema said, 'So you work in insurance?' and laughed meaninglessly for the sixth time, and Keshav was entangling her further in the search for something in a tasteless, colourless life.

'And?' she said with a deep breath.

And Keshav looked at her with vacant eyes, then turned his gaze towards the darkness outside.

'You mustn't have eaten anything at Kapoor's, should I get something cooked? The problem is that I'm not eating anything tonight—otherwise dinner would be ready.'

'Not at all, no-no.'

'Tea?'

'Mmmmhhmm.'

Then they silently drew so close to each other that Prema got up awkwardly—'let's see'. Keshav lit a cigarette and readily started going over the details of the past five years. He had almost forgotten Prema. His masculine pride had constrained him to actually forget Prema. He was wondering why he hadn't come before, by chance, here, where his horns could so easily pierce, and doesn't Prema move too quickly with the circle of time? He came out onto the verandah. Saw Prema sitting still as a statue. In the uncertainty of darkness, she heard his footsteps and stood up. She laughed, and Keshav felt this laugh tingle in his spine; he silently drew closer. Perhaps he wanted to see, he wanted to see her soul's rock bottom, but this is what we think. Prema switched on the light and in the sharp, flat electric glow, her face for a moment turned lacklustre.

'Here, insure me,' she laughed again.

And Keshav, incensed, threw away the cigarette after sucking on it twice.

They sat down; silence again but it was as though Keshav found himself again in an instant.

'Who knew (deep breath) that we would meet again like this (stop)!'

'Meet again'. . . it was as if she wanted to chew not the sound of these words but their massed bodies, with her teeth. Keshav felt quite helpless.

'Prema'—his voice held a strangeness but she was neither startled by this strangeness nor intrigued by it.

'Prema, how many children do you have?'—as if it was just to ask this question that Keshav had become a slave to words. As if he had an indisputable right to ask such a question. Prema said plainly—'One', 'No', like she was refusing the trump in some ordinary game of cards.

'One, no'—he was surprised by a curious contentment, as if he had asked this question only to receive this answer, then said, 'Are you not happy?'

'Happy,' she said as if she didn't understand anything.

'Prema'—now Keshav was fixing his course, a marvellous discontent was agitating him. He placed the chair against the wall. He put out his hand wanting to touch her cool, fair arms, yes, touch, and it seemed to him that this had no force at all, not at all; but Prema was silent in body and soul, it was not that she deliberately wanted to keep Keshav at a distance, it was not that her heart was being wasted, in these special circumstances, she had forgotten even her 'baby', as if she'd never had a child—as if, in life, it was so easy to return somewhere from somewhere else. She laughed just like that and said—'Why did you ask about children?'

Keshav wanted to answer with a smile but quickly turned serious and said, 'Well . . . who are you knitting this sweater for? Are you . . .'

Prema suddenly became very dramatic. Her face lit up. Flowers bloomed in her eyes and she exclaimed 'dhut!' and sprang towards the room.

Keshav abruptly got up and quickly held her hand. Uff, her hands were so cool; he let go of them in the space of a moment. Prema understood, understood him completely. His holding her hands and, even more, his letting go of them.

She went inside the room, closed the door and said in an extremely matter-of-fact voice—

'I am sleeping, you should sleep, too. Make your bed. The servants won't enter.'

Keshav—silent.

Prema: 'Are you asleep?'

Keshav: 'Prema!'

Prema: 'Go to sleep.'

Keshav (emotionally): 'Prema, come here.'

Prema; 'I am already asleep.'

Keshav silent—silent—silent, as if he was forgetting everything relevant in this slow wave, as if all the bonds surrounding him wanted to set him free, and at a distance, a woman, strange-strange, but no definite impression of her strangeness was reaching his mind. He said, collecting himself, "Prema, I can't sleep. Come, let's talk about something.'

'Talk about what?'—Prema said, fully awake, 'something?'

'Something,' Prema repeated mechanically.

'No,' she paused, 'I have taken off my saree.' Keshav was silent, he had found a reason to be silent. His mind was searching for her and a strange lassitude extinguished his limbs, and after growing de-centred, weightless, either he became fervid or she left the realm of his life—he kept sitting there, stunned, and then fell on to the chair and passed out.

In the morning, the servant awoke Prema. She called out, 'Bahu rani!' from the window. Prema woke up. Sticky, tired eyes, swollen. Lips twisted, the servant asked, 'That gentleman left so early in the morning?' Suddenly, looking into her eyes, she saw it all. Keshav had left behind a letter, a heavy blue envelope. She turned it over several times and then placed it in a trunk, unopened. She was rather glum all day and carried on knitting the sweater. In the evening, she didn't get up even when she heard her husband's voice. He walked in, and said, 'Here's your little prince, see if I have harmed him' and then laughed a little, not wanting to sound too sharp. After he'd bathing and changed, he saw the child wrapped around Prema's legs while she kept on mechanically knitting the sweater. He sat on the armrest of her chair, pulled her close and asked, 'What happened, you seem very angry?' She didn't stop, didn't hesitate, just turned a dry, melancholy face towards him and said, 'Keshav.'

'Did Keshav come here?' He asked in a casual tone, with a touch of impatience.

'No,' she said, looking into her husband's deep blue eyes, then: 'Yes, I kept dreaming about him all night as if he had died—leave it.' Her husband interrupted her: 'Am I not good enough for death?' and he kissed her face, both lips, both corners; but today she was thirsting for some unknown essence. Her soul, parched, wanted to be weightless and float in the void.

Anyway, all this is just poetry.

POSTMASTER

It is difficult to say how long it has been since he started sitting like a weary traveller of stony paths, under the dense shade of a tamarind tree, there where two roads met. In the language of fiction, it may be said 'since forever' but he was surrounded by such immense peace that all imagination stalled at its sight. As if—after reaching the end point of liquid imagination, he was mocking it resolutely and bitterly.

He would arrive with his arched back, his walking stick made of nagfani wood, his soiled knee-length coat, his pair of glasses tied with thread, his bag under his arm, and sit on his dirty, red-and-black stained bedding with some money-order forms, a few plain envelopes, old letters and newspapers filled with images.

He was called the postmaster and was, by vocation, an old letter writer. It was so that once, during 'war times', when the real postmaster had installed him in his chair and gone off to see his fiancée in another village without taking leave, that people had started calling him 'postmaster'. And the vivid, powerful memories of how he had bossed around the postmen, rebuked even the seniors, and once even slapped a drunken white man, had become an essential part of his life. In reality, he had reached that stage when one starts believing one's own delusions. No one except him remembered that the postman's business once used to run well . . . and these days when he had to borrow even the evening's tobacco, some friend or stranger . . .

Anyway, he had thought deeply about the subject. And had achieved only a kind of indifference from all this unexpected philosophy. He was lonely, that wasn't so important; but his life had shrunk to his bed and the tiled roof of his small room in the ghetto and this lack had infused a strangeness and bitterness in his life that could, in all justice, in his particular context be deemed only 'indifference'. But Cheena? This is where his life was stuck, this was the point at which he stopped and looked at everything.

In the midst of the boys' shouts and hullabaloo, women's curses and abuses and lovers' kisses in broad daylight, the postmaster had scribbled Cheena's name on a clean sheet of paper and, with his broken pen-box, set up a village council. The accusation was that Cheena had run away from her in-laws' home. After listening to both sides, making an issue of cross-examination, the judgment rendered by him wasn't accepted by either party. Cheena didn't listen because of her burgeoning youth, bright dusky complexion, the poison and nectar of her eyes. She was an alcoholic milkman's niece, and bounced life around like a ball, glared at men, cursed and was cursed by the women, but she ran away from her in-laws for some rather ordinary reason: 'she ran away from her in-laws'.

And that night, the postmaster, lying on his ragged mattress, was staring at this sharp truth with his eyes wide open.

When the pace of life quickens, it turns into something like ease. It seems that we have conquered our bonds and boundaries, we have moved on from struggle, but this is a difficult delusion. We don't realize it and neither did the poor postmaster.

He had no tangible relationship with Cheena. He certainly couldn't imagine a fictional relationship—but we can assure you that even if he did think about Cheena, it was dispassionately, with neutrality.

In the evenings, on his way back home, he would always look at Cheena, staring innocently, laughing merrily or bruising someone with her words; but her every mood would have the same effect on him and he would return home, close the door carefully, and, when the little room would grow enchanted with smoke from the stove, he would rub his eyes and say: 'That bitch.'

A wanton fury inhabited his life, and he saw how it made incoherent all things around him. When he couldn't sleep at night, he would reflect on his childhood, sometimes a faraway incident of his youth would hurt him; and one night he suddenly thought of the distant relative with whom he had stayed during the last Kumbh, and his daughter—he even remembered her name, Rammi—fair, slender, shy; for no reason at all, he was unexpectedly inspired to think that she was not a 'virgin', and he got up and began to cough.

Many times, he decided to reason with Cheena. Why? We are certain that if he reflected on it, he would be inhibited by the sheer pointlessness of the reason; but he paused many times when he found her alone, returning from the market or branding the calves; but despite trying many times, he couldn't utter a word and merely watched her laugh a gross, careless laugh. He would get irritated again, and on those days argue with his customers.

Imagination is resistance against life and nature. We try to remain above life's pettiness and chains, riding on the shadow-wings of our minute and microcosmic feelings and empathies and, for a time, forget our real, trouble-filled life. The postmaster did the same. When did he do this? To know this, we would have to reach into his deepest subconscious, from where this entire business seems like a cruel joke; but by painting Cheena in the colours of his imagination, he benefitted from a sense of ease. He breathed a sigh of relief at allotting her a fixed place. Now he could look at Cheena with an immense sympathy, think about her husband, who, perpetually drunk, must be insulting her regularly, he could meditate on the shameless prostitute who must make Cheena's life hell—sometimes he actually choked up at these thoughts. Once, he even found a place in his imagination for the khadi-clad youth who had stayed here for a few days under the pretext of reform and was spotted flirting with a few girls. Who knows why but he thought that youth was the reason behind her leaving; but this imaginary misconduct disturbed him again and that day, sitting in his shop, when he saw Cheena pass by, a bale of straw on her head, he felt a tingling. When she returned after selling the straw, she lowered her eyes, smiled and approached the postmaster hoping to get a letter written.

'Hindi-Urdu postcard four paise, five paise for half-tola envelope, six paise for one-tola envelope. One anna for money order, go there for telegrams, speak clearly.'

Like a machine the postmaster babbled the same words he repeated so many times a day.

Cheena made him swear on 'Ganga mother' and 'cow mother' and dictated a letter to a daroga in her husband's town, and the postmaster wrote and posted it. Cheena bound him by oath once again, smiled and flounced off; but the postmaster—it was as if he came undone, as if he was beginning life all over again. As if he was an unwelcome guest from his last life. And that evening, on his way home, when a boy stopped him to ask for a coin, he suddenly turned nasty and hissed like a wounded snake: 'Swine!'

No one had seen him like that before.

WAR

The train left Chandpur a full twenty-five minutes late. The PWI trolley was being loaded and the abject face of the stationmaster passed our window. The khadi-clad man skilfully folded his newspaper, began to fan himself and stuck his face outside the window. The gorkha soldier brought his luggage down and arranged it for the third time. Tall military bags that could be locked, a trunk with a fading pattern of yellow creepers, bedding tied with leather belts and a Nepali basket, he was perhaps returning from leave— wiping the rifle clean, then putting it down, he was reciting 'Manzil aur Butts' in a slow, mumbling voice—he held the gun as if it were a wild beast tamed by infirmity . . . the train did hoon-hoon-hoon as it waited for a signal . . . and the whole compartment started to hum. Outside, the distant deep-blue trees looked like small hills, the train's lights weren't on yet. The khadi-clad man leant far out of the window and said almost to himself, 'There's no signal.' In the corner, the student folded his wrinkled achkan, placed it under his head, gazed at the roof and blew out rings of smoke. He was making strange faces like a clown. Whenever he managed a particularly good ring, he would look victoriously at the woman in the corner of the bench opposite. The woman's husband had dozed off but was now trying to stay awake after being startled by the train's halting. He stared for a full minute at the child sitting quietly, then suddenly asked his wife, 'Inder's wife's dad'll be in Khatauli? Or she'll go to her husband herself?' His voice had a needless harshness. The woman reluctantly bobbed her head in uncertain answer—the train moved, and she turned to look outside after covering her legs with her saree.

The khadi-clad man yawned and snapped his ringed fingers—chhat, chhat, chhat. The student's cigarette was finished, and he took out his wallet and began counting his money.

It grew darker and the lights still weren't switched on. The student, placing the wallet back in his pocket, said, 'Thieves, bloody thieves.' The khadi-clad man looked at him, gave a superior smile, then turned his face away. It was as if the darkness was flowing from outside into the train. People's faces had faded, the soldier had spread his bedding and was now phat-phat-phat smoothing its wrinkles. The boy, standing on his bench, was looking at him with a strange longing. The soldier arranged the bedding and looked at the boy. In an attempt to make him and, more so his mother, laugh, he began to make faces like a folk performer.

The khadi-clad man finally asked, 'Which regiment are you in?'

'146 Gurkha Rifles.'

But the soldier was already busy with the child.

'Where is your regiment?'

'In Mhow Cantt.'

'War is about to begin,' the student said, lighting a cigarette.

The khadi-clad man again gave that knowing smile, the woman's husband who had dozed off again woke up and started coughing. Pulling the boy away from the window, he said to the woman, 'Devi from Sardhana has taken a contract for grass in Meerut.'

The woman, scratching her waist, said with a serious expression, 'Yes.'

The soldier was saying . . . he will soon get a pension—I was in Durbar Singh's regiment, the same Durbar Singh who got the Victoria Cross . . .

The woman's husband said, 'If there is a war, Devi will become a big man, the biggest is Colonel Miharwan, who . . .' The woman, yawning, said, 'Make a contract with the military now, now's a good time . . .' The soldier was waving his small, yellow, wrinkled hands in the air and saying something, 'In the year '14, four nations placed a rifle in these hands so that animals with hands and feet like ours could be hunted . . .' The woman denounced with some relish, 'What use is this Gandhiji's renown . . . Gandhi has erected his own mills . . .' The child was roaming the compartment, counting the windows again and again. The khadi-clad man removed the child from in front of him, looked at the woman and then gave his superior smile.

The student said loudly, 'But why did you go to war, what did you get, some shiny buttons, uniforms stripped from dead bodies, heat, gonorrheal debauched nurses?' . . . The soldier (the compartment was now lit with a dull blue light) was protesting strongly, 'German hospitals . . . trenches . . . besides the English are a forgetful lot.'

And I dozed off with my head on the window.

Woke up. There was a bright, warm light in the compartment, the khadi-clad man had disembarked, the woman and her husband were asleep, the student was blowing the same rings of smoke. The boy was sitting on the soldier's bedding, he had collected the cigarette butts. He was counting them.

One, two, three . . . five.

There were ten in all.

WOLVES

'What's a wolf?' Kharu gypsy said, 'I'm the only one from Panethi who can kill a wolf.' I believed him. Kharu was scared of nothing, and, although he was almost seventy, and a lifetime of poverty had dimmed his appearance, you still believed him when he spoke like this. His real name was Iftikhar or something like that but the shortened Kharu suited him. He was surrounded by just such an incomprehensible and impenetrable hardness. His eyes were cold and frozen and, under the thick white moustache, his mouth was as inhuman and pitiless as a rat-trap.

He was done with life and death didn't want him, yet still he survived, spitting in the face of time. Unconcerned about your opinion, good or bad, he never told a lie and it was as if he showed, with his own merciless bitter truth, how barren and terrifying the truth can be. Kharu told me this story and I cannot describe in words the convincing manner and complete indifference with which it was told. But I believe it to be true, every word of it.

'I am not scared of anything, yes, except for wolves, I am not scared of anything,' Kharu said. 'Not just one wolf, not two or four.

A pack of two hundred or three hundred that emerges on winter nights, whose hunger cannot be satisfied with all the things of all the world, those wolves—no one can face that army of demons. People say a lone wolf is a coward. This is a lie. A wolf is never a coward—even alone, it is always alert. If you think foxes are cunning, it's because you don't know wolves. Have you ever seen a wolf hunt—a swamp deer? It doesn't overact like a lion, or show off like a bear. Once, just once, the wolf bounds up like a ball and slashes a deep wound in the thigh—that's it. Then it follows, from a distance, the trail of dripping blood to where the weakened deer has finally collapsed. Or, it springs on to an animal three times its size, gashes its stomach—and latches on to it. The wolf is a dangerously cunning and courageous animal. It never tires. Good-quality bulls can pull our gypsy caravans faster than horses but when they smell a wolf, they don't just run—they fly. But no four-footed animal can run faster than a wolf.'

'Listen, I was on my way back from Gwalior. It was unusually cold and the wolf packs were already out. Our caravan was rather heavy. Me, my father, my household, three girl acrobats—fifteen, fifteen, fifteen years old. We were taking them . . .'

'For what?'

'What do you think—to perform? To sell, of course! They have no other value. Girl acrobats from Gwalior are usually quite plump and sell well in Punjab. These girls were quite delicious but also quite heavy We had one fast gypsy caravan and three bulls that could run faster than horses.

'We had left at dawn, because we wanted to meet up with our partners in daylight. And we were carrying two bows and a gun for protection. The bulls were running spiritedly and we had already covered 20 miles when the old man turned and said, "Kharu, wolves?"

'I said quickly, "What? There are wolves? If there were, wouldn't the bulls know?"

'The old man shook his head and said, "No, there are definitely wolves. Anyway, they're about 10 miles behind us, but the bulls are tired and we still have 50 miles to go. And I know these wolves. Last year, they ate up a few prisoners—they devoured everything but the chains and police guns. Load the gun."

'I tested the bows, snapped open the gun, everything was fine.

'"Also check the new pack of gunpowder," my father said.

'"Pack of gunpowder?" I said,"I only have the old one."

'Then the old man started abusing me, "You . . . you . . ."

'I searched the whole caravan but there was no new packet.

'My father also searched. "You're lying, you wolf-child, I gave you the new pack." But that gunpowder was not there. My father elbowed me in the back and said, "I'll skin you alive when we reach the city, when we reach the city . . ."

'Right at that moment the bulls suddenly paused, then swished their tails and bolted. I heard a sound from miles away, faint like the sound of wind moving in ancient ruins—

'Hwa aa aa aa aa aa aa aa aa!

'"Wind," I said fearfully. '"Wolves," my father said in disgust, and took the bulls in hand. But they didn't need the whip. They had smelt the wolves and were running as fast as they could. I could see a black stain stir at a distance. You could see anything from miles away in that flat, barren, endless desert. And I could see that black stain move towards us like a cloud. The old man said, "As soon as they come near us, shoot. If you waste even one arrow, I'll rip out your liver." The three girls clung to each other and started crying. "Shut up," I said, "You make a sound and I'll toss you out."

'The wolves were advancing, we were flying across the brown stony earth—but the wolves! The old man gave up the reins and sat cradling the gun. I held the bow: I could hunt flying drakes in the dark and as for my father—once he took aim at something, even Allah had to forget about it. From a distance of about 400 yards, my father felled the first wolf. Bang! It somersaulted once like an acrobat and then again a second time. The bulls were running like mad, the froth from their mouths showering our faces like rain. And they were bellowing like gypsy women do when they imitate cattle in heat. And they kept coming closer. The pack swallowed the dead wolves without a pause, then swept over them. My father rested the gun barrel on my shoulder. Bang! Bang! (My shoulder still bears the scar of the burn.) I killed sixteen wolves with sixteen arrows, the old man killed ten, but the circle kept coming closer and closer.

'"Here, hold the gun," he said, "I'll handle the bulls."

'He believed the bulls could run even faster but he was wrong. No bull in the world could run faster than that.

'I was quite good with guns too but this was a local, rusted one. Anyway, the girl Baandi could refill it within five minutes.

She was a good girl, she would fill the gun and I would shoot—perfectly. I felled ten more—bang—bang—bang! By the time the gunpowder was finished, the wolves had started to look a little defeated.

'I said, "Now they've fallen behind."

'The old man laughed, "They won't fall behind so easily. But, I will now swear with my dying breath that Kharu is the best marksman among all the gypsies of the seven continents."

'My father had become quite the jester in his old age.

'So, the wolves had fallen a little behind. They had found something to eat. The whip was moving swish-swish-snap on the bulls when, within five minutes, the wolves returned. They were only about 200 yards away and getting closer. My father said, "Throw away the things, lighten the caravan."

'The caravan stumbled once, then sped up. Our caravan was the best in the gypsy colony, and now, without its load, it was as light as a flower, and for some time it seemed that we had, indeed, left the wolves behind—but they soon returned.

'The old man said, "Now, let one of the bulls loose."

'"What?" I asked, "Can only two bulls pull the caravan?"

'He said, "OK, then throw out a girl." I picked up the fat one and swung her outside. Ha. An acrobat from Gwalior! She can fight even the wolves if provoked. First she ran but then realizing it was futile, she turned to face them and gripped the first wolf by its legs. But that was equally futile. She suddenly disappeared. As if she had fallen into a well. The caravan, lighter now, moved forward, but the wolves returned again.

'"Toss out another one," the old man said. I protested, "We don't really travel for pleasure, do we? Why not just untie a bull."

'I untied another bull. It bellowed and ran, its tail across its back. The circle turned towards it.

'My father got all teary. "A noble bull, a noble bull . . ." he kept murmuring.

'At least we're safe," I said. But just then: Hwa aa aa aa aa aa! The circle had returned. "It's Judgement Day," I said and made the bulls gallop so fast that my hands started dripping blood.

'But the wolves were flowing towards us like water, and our bulls were about to collapse. "Throw out the second girl!" my father screamed.

'Baandi was the heavier of the two and, thinking something or the other, she began to remove her silver nose-ring with trembling hands. And maybe I didn't tell you but I used to quite like her.

'That's why I said to the other girl, "You, get out!" But it was as if she was paralysed. I threw her out and she remained lying the way she fell. The caravan was now even lighter and started moving faster. But the wolves came back after 5 miles. The old man took a deep breath and lamented, "What can we do, it's our destiny as gypsies to be beggars but we wanted to be rich . . ."

'I looked at Baandi. She looked at me. I said, "Will you jump or should I push you?" She removed the silver nose-ring, handed it to me, covered her eyes with her arms and jumped. The caravan now flew like the wind. It was the best gypsy caravan.

'But our bulls were exhausted and the colony was still 30 miles away. I kept shooting them dead but the wolves kept coming back.

'Sweat was streaming from my father's face. "Let's untie the second bull."

'I said, "It will be like jumping into the jaws of death. We'll both die. At least one of us should survive."

'"You're right," he said. "I'm an old man. My life has ended. I will jump."

'I said, "Don't be sad. If I stay alive, I'll butcher each and every wolf."

'"My noble son!" My father said and kissed me on both cheeks. Then took two big knives in both hands and wrapped a piece of cloth tightly around his throat.

'"Wait," he said, "I'm wearing new shoes. They would have lasted me another ten years. But look, don't wear these. Dead men's shoes should never be worn. Just sell them."

'He pulled off his shoes, flung them into the caravan and jumped into the middle of wolves. I didn't look back but for some time I could hear him scream, "Here you go! Here! You wolf-child! You wolf-child!" And then—slurp-slurp, slurp-slurp. Only I was somehow saved.'

Kharu looked at my frightened face, laughed loudly, hawked and spat copiously on the ground.

'The next year, I killed sixty of those wolves,' he then said, laughing. But an ominous hardness flashed in his eyes and, hungry and naked, he rose straight to his feet.

A List of Sources

'Sun Worship'
'*Suryapuja*', 1939. First published in *Hans* (July–August 1939).

'A Glimpse of Life'
'*Jeevan Ki Jhalak*', 1935. First published in *Hans* (May 1935).

'Alas, the Human Heart!'
'*Hai Re, Manav Hriday!*' 1935. First published in *Hans* (March 1935).

'Aunty'
'*Mausi*', 1934. First published in *Hans* (October 1934).

'Freedom: A Letter'
'*Azaadi: Ek Patra*', 1941. First published in *Chaand* (July 1941).

'In the Womb of the Future'
'*Bhavishya Ke Garbh Mein*'. Undated. First published in *Kahaani–Paakshik*.

'Masterni'
'*Masterni*', 1938. First published in *Chakallas* (May 1938).

'Mother and Sons'
'*Maa–Bete*', 1937. First published in *Hans* (April 1937).

'One Night'
'*Ek Raat*', 1936. First published in *Hans* (June 1936).

'Postmaster'
'*Daakmunshi*', 1935. First published in *Hans* (June 1935).

'War'
'*Ladaai*', 1939. First published in *Hans* (September 1939).

'Wolves'
'*Bhediye*', 1938. First published in *Hans* (April 1938).